Purr-ty in Pink

PuRRMaiDS

The Scaredy Cat
The Catfish Club
Seasick Sea Horse
Search for the Mermicorn
A Star Purr-formance
Quest for Clean Water
Kittens in the Kitchen
Merry Fish-mas
Kitten Campout
A Grrr-eat New Friendship
A Purr-fect Pumpkin
Party Animals

MeRMicoRns®

Sparkle Magic
A Friendship Problem
The Invisible Mix-Up
Sniffles and Surprises

Purr-ty in Pink

by Sudipta Bardhan-Quallen

illustrations by Vivien Wu

A STEPPING STONE BOOK™
Random House 🏠 New York

Text copyright © 2023 by Sudipta Bardhan-Quallen
Cover art copyright © 2023 by Andrew Farley
Interior illustrations copyright © 2023 by Vivien Wu

Random House and the colophon are registered trademarks and A Stepping Stone Book and the colophon are trademarks of Penguin Random House LLC. PURRMAIDS® is a registered trademark of KIKIDOODLE LLC and is used under license from KIKIDOODLE LLC.

Visit us on the Web!
rhcbooks.com

Educators and librarians, for a variety of teaching tools, visit us at
RHTeachersLibrarians.com

Library of Congress Cataloging-in-Publication Data
Names: Bardhan-Quallen, Sudipta, author. | Wu, Vivien, illustrator.
Title: Purr-ty in pink / by Sudipta Bardhan-Quallen; illustrated by Vivien Wu.
Description: First edition. | New York: Random House Children's Books, [2023] |
Series: Purrmaids; 13 | Audience: Ages 6–9. | Summary: Shelly, Coral, and Angel visit
Flamingo Island with Shelly's mom, but Shelly must put things right when the rock
she took as a keepsake ends up being a flamingo egg.
Identifiers: LCCN 2022042655 (print) | LCCN 2022042656 (ebook) |
ISBN 978-0-593-64534-5 (trade paperback) |
ISBN 978-0-593-64535-2 (library binding) | ISBN 978-0-593-64536-9 (ebook)
Subjects: CYAC: Mermaids—Fiction. | Cats—Fiction. |
Flamingos—Fiction. | Eggs—Fiction.
Classification: LCC PZ7.B25007 Pv 2023 (print) | LCC PZ7.B25007 (ebook) |
DDC [Fic]—dc23

Printed in the United States of America
10 9 8 7 6 5 4 3 2 1
First Edition

This book has been officially leveled by using
the F&P Text Level Gradient™ Leveling System.

To Tesla,
a paw-sitively purr-fect fan

1

It was a bright and beautiful Saturday morning in Kittentail Cove. That meant there was no sea school today. Even though it was a weekend, a kitten with white, silky fur named Shelly was already awake. She was waiting to see her best friends!

Shelly floated to the doorway of her house. She poked her head out and looked up and down the street. There were other purrmaids swimming all around. But she couldn't see any black-and-white kittens or any orange-striped kittens. *Where are Angel and Coral?*

"Maybe they're not coming," someone purred.

"Maybe they changed their minds," someone else said.

Shelly felt two paws ruffling her fur. She turned around to face her twin sisters, Tempest and Gale. They were always teasing her. Most of the time, it wasn't so bad. Big sisters were like that. Today, though, Shelly was worried that her sisters might be right. There were already butterfly fish fluttering in her tummy.

Even worse, Tempest and Gale had made a mess of Shelly's fur. Shelly hated having a single strand out of place!

"Quit it, you two," Shelly mumbled. She smoothed her fur back into place.

"Are you wearing that new top for a reason?" Tempest asked.

"That color reminds me of something," Gale added.

"I know!" Tempest said. "It's the same color as Fluffy!"

"I remember Fluffy," Gale said. "Shelly couldn't sleep without him."

Fluffy was a flamingo toy Shelly got when she was a little kitten. Mom had brought back flamingo feathers from a trip to Flamingo Island. She used them to make Fluffy, 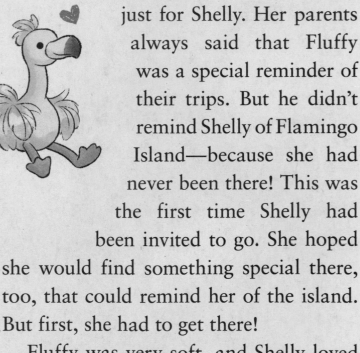 just for Shelly. Her parents always said that Fluffy was a special reminder of their trips. But he didn't remind Shelly of Flamingo Island—because she had never been there! This was the first time Shelly had been invited to go. She hoped she would find something special there, too, that could remind her of the island. But first, she had to get there!

Fluffy was very soft, and Shelly loved

to snuggle him at bedtime. Shelly's sisters liked to tease her about that, too.

"Yes, this top is flamingo pink," Shelly replied.

"Look!" Gale said. "There are flamingos on the pocket!"

"Those flamingos look like Fluffy," Tempest said. "Are you bringing Fluffy to Flamingo Island?"

Shelly didn't want to say that she had packed Fluffy for the trip. *They'll never stop making fun of me!* Before she could think of what to say, someone else floated up.

"You don't need to know what Shelly is bringing," Mom said, "because you two are not coming." She put one paw on Tempest's shoulder and the other on Gale's. "You are the big sisters. Don't tease Shelly."

"Sorry, Mom," Tempest mumbled.

"Sorry, Shelly," Gale added.

Shelly crossed her paws over her chest and grinned. She watched her sisters swim toward the kitchen. But when they disappeared around the corner, Shelly's grin faded. She peeked out the door again.

"I love that color on you," Mom purred. "And the girls will be here soon."

Shelly frowned. "They're late! I've been waiting fur-ever!" She played with her friendship bracelet. Coral and Angel had matching ones. All the charms reminded them of the adventures they had together. But now they just reminded Shelly that her friends weren't there. "They wouldn't change their minds, would they?" Shelly asked. "Tempest and Gale said they might have."

Mom smiled. "They wouldn't change their minds," she replied.

"I just want this trip to be paw-some," Shelly said. She glanced up at the clock and scowled. "But Coral and Angel are late. So maybe everything is already messed up."

Mom pulled Shelly into a hug. "This trip will be fun," she said, "because we are

going with purrmaids we love. Even if we have to change the plan or fix mistakes!"

Shelly sighed. "I know that," she said.

"And your friends aren't late," Mom continued. "They said they'd come over *after* breakfast. We haven't eaten yet!"

Shelly scratched her head. "I forgot that part."

"Which part?" Mom asked. "That they're coming after breakfast or that you haven't had breakfast?"

"Both!" Shelly said as her tummy rumbled.

2

There was a small container on the kitchen counter. It was filled with the last of the sweet shrimp. "There wasn't enough to use at the restaurant today," Mom said. "I thought we'd finish it for breakfast."

"That way there will be plenty of room for the fresh shrimp we'll bring back from Flamingo Island!" Shelly said, laughing.

Shelly's family ran a wonderful

restaurant in Kittentail Cove. They used shrimp in many recipes. Mr. Lake made shrimp rolls, shrimp and tuna-egg omelets, and shrimp salad. Mrs. Lake made shrimp sushi, shrimp and coconut sandwiches, and shrimp tacos. Shelly had created a very special recipe called Mango and Mustard Shrimp Curry. It was one of the most popular meals on the menu!

The Lakes got their shrimp from a very special place—Flamingo Island. Flamingos loved eating shrimp. There were lots of shrimp to feast on around their island. That made it a great place for purrmaids to get shrimp, too!

Mr. and Mrs. Lake camped out at Flamingo Island for a night to gather fresh shrimp for the restaurant. But they couldn't catch too many shrimp on any trip. So they had to go back every few months.

"Are you paying attention, Shelly?" Tempest asked.

"I don't think so!" Gale said.

"I'm sorry," Shelly purred. "I didn't hear you."

"Mom said come to the table," Tempest said.

"And hurry up! We're starving!" Gale added.

"Shelly might be floating here in front of us," Mom said, "but I think her mind is far away on Flamingo Island."

Shelly grinned as she sat down at the table. "You're right," she said.

"I'm always right!" Mom joked. Then she asked, "Who wants kelp pancakes?"

All the girls answered at the same time. "Me!"

Mom served each of them a few pancakes topped with shrimp slices. For a few minutes, no one said anything. Their mouths were too full of food! When Mom got up to get more pancakes, Tempest said, "You know, Shelly, it takes a long time to get to Flamingo Island."

Shelly rolled her eyes.

"We mean a really, really long

time," Gale said. "Are you leaving after breakfast?"

"If Angel and Coral get here," Shelly answered.

Mom put another pancake on Shelly's plate. "Stop worrying, Shelly! Your friends have never let you down, have they?"

Shelly shook her head. She put the last bite of food into her mouth and looked at the clock on the wall. She frowned. "But they're officially late now!"

Just then, the doorbell rang. "They're here!" Shelly cried. She swam over and opened the door. She immediately asked, "What took you so long?"

Angel giggled. "Coral made us go to the library," she said. She pointed to a heavy book in Coral's paws.

"Yes," Coral said, "but you already made us late leaving your house!"

In the kitchen, Mom exclaimed, "Finally! We were starting to worry." She winked at Shelly. "And we need to get moving. We don't want to miss our ride."

"Ride?" Angel asked. "Aren't we swimming to Flamingo Island?"

"Surprise!" Shelly exclaimed. "I didn't

tell you this before, but you can't get to Flamingo Island by swimming."

Coral and Angel frowned. "How do purrmaids get around without swimming?" Coral asked.

Shelly grinned. "Have you ever heard of a submarine?"

Now the other two kittens' eyes grew wide. "We're riding a submarine?" Angel asked.

"Yes!" Shelly answered. "But we have to hurry. The captain says he leaves on time, no matter what!"

3

Shelly, Angel, Coral, and Mom grabbed their backpacks and the shrimp traps.

"Why only four traps?" Angel asked. "Couldn't we catch more shrimp with more traps?"

"I know why!" Coral exclaimed. "There's a chapter in my library book about it. It's because taking too many shrimp away from Flamingo Island can . . ." Her voice trailed off. She shrugged. "I haven't finished the chapter yet."

"Coral is right," Mom said. "Trapping too much shrimp isn't a good idea. Most of the animals who live on Flamingo Island eat shrimp."

"So if we take too many, those animals won't have enough food?" Shelly asked.

Mom nodded. "Four full shrimp traps let us make lots of shrimp-filled food here in Kittentail Cove. But that still leaves enough shrimp for the other animals."

Coral purred, "I loved the shrimp tacos you made for us after sea school last week, Mrs. Lake."

"Me too!" Angel added. "I wish we could have more right now."

Mom said, "We go through shrimp

purr-ty quickly." She grinned. "But that just means more trips to Flamingo Island!"

Shelly giggled. "We have to go on our *first* trip before there can be *more*!"

The Great Neptune Current was one of the fastest currents in the ocean. It was too dangerous for purrmaids to ride by themselves! The water moved so fast that someone on their own could get bumped and rattled! So purrmaids didn't just swim into the Great Neptune Current. They rode on the Trident submarine!

The purrmaids hurried to the entrance. But where was the Trident? Shelly couldn't see it anywhere. But she did see a sign. "The Trident is this way," she announced.

Mom pointed to a large, plain building. "That's the submarine shed."

"I bet that's the captain," Shelly said.

"I've been waiting for you!" Mr. Nemo shouted, waving.

"Hello, Mr. Nemo," Mom called. "It's so nice to see you."

"You too!" Mr. Nemo replied. "I'm looking forward to taking you back to

Flamingo Island. But first, tell me who you've brought with you."

Mom smiled. "This is my daughter Shelly," she said. "And these are her best friends, Angel and Coral. This is their first trip to Flamingo Island."

"Then it's an exciting day!" Mr. Nemo exclaimed. He floated over to the submarine and called, "All aboard!"

The captain led everyone to the control room. The steering wheel was on one side of the room. There was a window on the other side with a bench in front of it. The long wall was made up of a line of cabinets.

"It's important that everything aboard a submarine is stowed properly," Mr.

Nemo explained. "The Trident can take really fast turns. So if there's anything lying around, it could glide through the water. It could even hit someone!" He pulled his sleeve up and showed them a bandage. "I learned that the hard way. I had a little accident on my last trip!"

"We don't want that to happen again," Angel said.

"To any of us!" Coral added.

Mr. Nemo lifted up the seat of the bench. "The shrimp traps fit purr-fectly in here," he said. "Your bags go in a cabinet."

"This one?" Coral asked. She pointed to the cabinet on the left end of the row. It was the only cabinet that had a large starfish hanging from the handle.

Mr. Nemo shook his head. He went to the other end of the row. He twisted the handle to the right and opened the door. "Put your stuff here."

When everything was packed, Mr. Nemo shut the cabinet door. "Let's keep this locked," he said. He turned the handle so it pointed down. Then he waved toward the bench. "Get comfortable, girls. Mrs. Lake and I will make sure everything is ready."

Shelly and Coral swam straight to the

bench. But Angel stayed floating near the cabinets.

"Come on, Angel," Shelly shouted. "You're never this slow!"

Angel frowned. "Did you guys see this?" she asked. She touched the hanging starfish.

"It's a starfish," Shelly said. "We see those everywhere."

"But Mr. Nemo told us everything on a

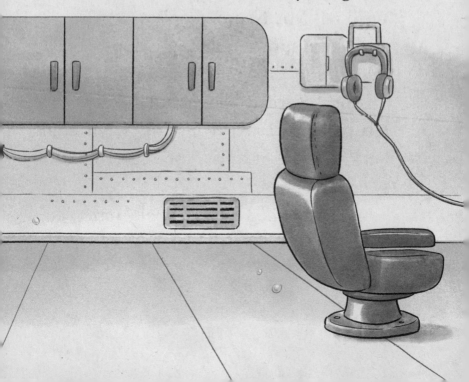

submarine needs to be stowed properly," Angel said. "This should be put away, too."

"I don't know, Angel," Coral said. "Maybe we shouldn't touch it without asking Mr. Nemo."

Angel shrugged. "I don't think we need to ask permission to clean up," she said. She grabbed the starfish and opened the door. "I'll put it on this shelf for now. We'll tell Mr. Nemo later."

"Make sure you lock the door," Shelly said.

Angel turned the handle down. She returned to her seat just as Mom came back. "All right, girls," she said, "put on your sea belts."

They snapped their sea belts into place. Angel said, "Now we're ready to go."

"And we can relax," Shelly added, "without worrying about how fast we're going."

"I like it when there's nothing to worry about!" Coral exclaimed.

4

Mr. Nemo steered the Trident slowly toward the Great Neptune Current. "Before we enter the current," he said, "we have to make sure there's nothing else in the way that we might bump into." He hit the brakes. The submarine stopped moving forward. The purrmaids all felt a little bounce. Luckily, their sea belts kept them from falling off the bench.

Unluckily, though, one of the cabinet doors fell open!

"Watch out!" Shelly exclaimed.

The purrmaids ducked. The door missed Angel's head by an inch!

"What happened?" Coral asked.

"I must not have locked the door properly," Angel answered.

Mr. Nemo went to the cabinets. He frowned and pointed to the handle. "Did someone move the starfish?" he asked.

Angel gulped. "I put it inside the cabinet," she said. "I thought it should be put away."

Mr. Nemo took out the starfish. He locked the handle and hung the starfish again. "It was a good idea," he said. "There's only one purr-oblem. This was hung here for a reason. Just watch." He took the starfish off the handle again. After a moment, the handle began to lift up.

"The door unlocked itself!" Shelly said.

Mr. Nemo smiled. "This handle is

broken. Hanging something heavy on it keeps it locked."

Angel looked down at her tail. "I thought I was doing the right thing," she said. "I'm sorry."

"It's all right, Angel," Mr. Nemo purred. "You tried to do the right thing. That's always a good idea. But even if something seems like a really good idea, it's better to ask questions if you can."

Angel nodded. "I guess something that looks like it doesn't matter can really be important."

"This is actually a good lesson to talk about," Mom said. "Angel has given us a purr-fect opportunity."

Angel grinned. "I knew I did something right—even while doing something wrong!"

"This is your first trip to Flamingo Island," Mr. Nemo continued. "We want you to have a fin-tastic time. But we also have to think about the critters who are already there."

"Purrmaids can visit the island," Mom

said, "but the flamingos *live* there. It's really important to respect their home while we are guests."

"That's why we won't take too many shrimp from the island," Shelly said.

"Exactly," Mr. Nemo said. "Leaving enough food for the animals of Flamingo Island is one way to be respectful. Another way is to make sure that nothing gets left behind that doesn't belong there."

"So we should clean up all our trash," Coral said.

"We always do that anyway!" Angel exclaimed. "Ms. Harbor taught us that it is important to keep the ocean clean for everyone."

"And," Coral continued, "we should ask before we touch, right?"

"Yes!" Mom replied.

"You girls might have other questions,"

Mr. Nemo said. "We can talk more while we travel. But for now, let's get the Trident moving again. We have a long way to go!"

The Trident inched forward onto the Great Neptune Current. It started slow. Then all of a sudden, they were zipping through the water! The ocean outside the window zoomed by the purrmaids' eyes.

Inside the Trident, it felt like they were sitting in Shelly's room. Shelly thought it was very relaxing.

"I never knew going fast could be this much fun!" Coral exclaimed.

"That's because you don't like going fast," Angel joked.

5

After a while, Mr. Nemo pulled a lever and announced, "Autopilot activated!" He swam to the window. There was a seat flipped up against the wall. He pulled it down and settled into it. He fastened his sea belt. Then he asked, "How does it feel, girls?"

"This is amazing!" Shelly said. "And so much easier than swimming the whole way would be."

Mr. Nemo chuckled. "Now, what other questions do you have about Flamingo Island?"

Shelly raised a paw. "I have one," she said. "Can we bring something home from Flamingo Island? Something to remind us of our trip?"

"Well," Angel replied, "we'll be bringing back a lot of shrimp!"

Shelly frowned. "I mean something that we won't eat right away."

Mom smiled. "We can't disturb the flamingos," she said. "Or any of the other animals on the island. After all, we are basically going to be floating around in their house."

"Would you like it if flamingos came to Kittentail Cove and took your stuff?" Mr. Nemo asked.

The girls giggled. "Flamingos can't

swim that deep underwater, can they?" Coral said.

"No," Mr. Nemo answered. "But still!"

"But can we collect something that the flamingos don't care about?" Shelly asked.

Mr. Nemo shrugged. "I suppose you could take something that you're paw-sitive the flamingos don't need."

Mom added, "But just to be safe, make sure you ask before you touch anything."

Coral and Angel asked more questions. But Shelly didn't really pay attention. She played with the friendship bracelet on her wrist. Many of the charms were made from things the girls had collected. Maybe the next charm would remind them of Flamingo Island.

Suddenly, Mr. Nemo pointed outside the window. "Look!" he said. "We're almost there."

Shelly looked up from her bracelet. "We are?" she asked. "I thought it took a really long time to get to Flamingo Island."

"It does," Mom replied. "We've been talking for a really long time!"

"And the Trident moves very fast!" Mr. Nemo added. He swam back to the steering wheel. "Get ready. We'll be stopping soon!"

Mr. Nemo put the Trident down on the ocean floor. "See those mangrove roots? That's how we know we've arrived."

"There's a whole forest of mangrove trees on the edge of the island," Mom added.

"Are you camping with us, Mr. Nemo?" Shelly asked.

"Not this time," Mr. Nemo replied. "But I'll be back tomorrow to pick you up. I can't wait to hear all about your stay!" He waved goodbye.

Then Coral asked, "Now that we're here, what are we going to do first?"

"See the flamingos, of course!" Shelly announced.

But Mom shook her head. "I know you're excited about the flamingos," she

purred. "But first we set up our camp.
Then we need to place the shrimp traps."

"Oh, Mom!" Shelly whined. "I've been
waiting to see the flamingos fur-ever!"

"I know, Shelly," Mom said. "But you'll have to wait just a little bit longer."

"Don't worry," Angel said. "We'll get everything done super quickly."

"We'll be wading in flamingo feathers before you know it!" Coral added.

Shelly smiled. She could always count on Coral and Angel to make things better. "Come on," she called. "Follow me!" She began to swim away. But then she stopped.

"What's wrong?" Coral asked.

Shelly shrugged. "I forgot that I don't actually know which way to go."

"Well, then," Mom said, laughing, "I guess you should follow me!"

6

The purrmaids swam to a patch of man-grove trees. Above the water's surface, the mangrove tree trunks split into a web of branches. Beneath the ocean, the roots spread out like underwater branches. That made them a purr-fect place to hang the hammocks.

"Tie the top of the hammock on one root," Mom explained. "Then stretch it out. But not too tight! You want it to be comfortable for sleeping."

Shelly tied one end of her hammock. Then she floated out far enough that the hammock curved down in the middle. "Is this good?" she asked.

"Purr-fect!" Mom replied. "Now tie the other end to a root over there."

Angel and Coral set up their hammocks on either side of Shelly's. "We're ready for our campout!" Coral said.

"But wait," Angel said. She looked in her backpack. "I think I forgot to pack a pillow."

Shelly checked her bag. She scratched her head. She had pajamas, clothes for tomorrow, and Fluffy. But nothing else. "I forgot to bring a pillow, too."

"Me too," Coral added, frowning.

Mom pawed through her bag. "I brought pillowcases and blankets for you girls. But I don't have extra pillows," she said. "You might all have to tough it out."

Coral and Angel frowned harder. But Shelly had a sudden idea. She took Fluffy out and placed him in her hammock.

When no one was looking, she took the pillowcases and stuffed them into her pocket. Then she said, "I guess there's nothing to be done. So we should probably go set up the shrimp traps." *After that,* she thought, *I can see if my plan will work!*

The purrmaids took the shrimp traps to a spot near the shore but far away from the flamingos. "That way we don't catch the shrimp that the flamingos were planning to eat," Mom said.

They placed the traps on the sand. Then they opened the doors so the shrimp could swim in. Mom slipped a small bag of bait inside each trap. "Tomorrow morning, these should be filled with shrimp!"

"That's it?" Angel asked.

Mom nodded and began to swim away.

"That was easy!" Coral exclaimed.

Shelly shouted, "Wait! Can we go see the flamingos now?"

Mom spun around to face the girls. "Where do you think I'm going?"

❧ ❧ ❧

The purrmaids swam past their campsite to another shallow area. "The flamingos live and play around here," Mom whispered. "Let's see where they are right now."

There were a few large rocks that rose out of the water. "Climb up," Mom said. "We can look through the gaps between these rocks."

Shelly peeked through the gap in front of her. To her right, there was a muddy area with mangrove trees on the far edge. There were pink feathers everywhere! *Those must be flamingo feathers,* Shelly thought. There were also little mounds everywhere. It looked like someone had made a whole lot of benches for flamingos to sit on. But there were no flamingos!

"Where are they?" Shelly asked.

Angel tapped Shelly's shoulder. She was looking through a gap in the rocks, too. But she was looking left. "Over here!" Angel cried.

Shelly turned and saw a long stretch of flat golden sand. But it wasn't empty sand. "The flamingos!" she exclaimed.

Some flamingos walked slowly on the beach. Others stood on one leg with their heads tucked under their wings. Some also walked in the shallow water. Every once in a while, they would dip their heads under the water. When they came back up, there were snacks in their beaks!

"Wow! They're so beautiful," Coral whispered.

"Can we get closer?" Angel asked.

Mom shook her head. "If we get too close to the flock, they will feel uncomfortable."

"That's what it said in my book," Coral said.

Shelly needed flamingo feathers to make her plan work. *But I want it to be a surprise.*

Then Shelly remembered what had happened on the Trident. *Angel thought it was right to move the starfish. But it needed to be there! She should have asked Mr. Nemo. He would have told her to leave it alone. Maybe that means I should ask Mom about my plan?*

Shelly pulled Mom to one side. "Can we get closer to that part, though?" she whispered. She pointed to the muddy area on the right.

"I guess that would be fine," Mom replied. "As long as the flamingos are over on the beach. But it would be hard to see the flamingos from there. Why would you want to go?"

She took the pillowcases out of her pocket. "I thought I could fill these with flamingo feathers to make pillows," Shelly whispered. "I want to surprise Coral and Angel! I think it's okay to take the feathers that have fallen on the ground. But I wanted to ask first."

Mom grinned. "You didn't need my permission to pick up the feathers on the ground!" She winked. "But now that I know, I can help you!"

7

Angel and Coral didn't even turn around when Shelly and Mom said they'd be right back. Her friends were only paying attention to the flamingos!

The water became very shallow as they got closer to the empty shore. "Flamingos *can* swim," Mom explained, "but they like to wade in the water more."

"What are those?" Shelly asked, looking at the mud mounds.

"Flamingo nests," Mom said. She pointed to the ground near the mounds. "Those are eggshells. Some babies must have hatched!"

"It would be *flam-azing* to see a flamingo baby!" Shelly said, winking.

Shelly and Mom floated around, scooping feathers into the pillowcases. When they'd filled them, Mom took the three new pillows. "I'll bring these back

to our campsite," she said. "You can go hang out at the rocks with your friends. Just come back to camp before it gets dark."

"Can I take one last look around here?" Shelly asked.

Mom nodded. "But don't stay too long," she said. "The flamingos wouldn't like anyone too close to their nests. So don't let them see you here."

"I'll be quick, I purr-omise," Shelly said, waving goodbye to Mom.

Shelly went closer to the shore. She wanted to get a better look at the nests. Most of them were too far from the edge of the water for her to explore easily. But there was one that she could swim up to. She discovered the mounds weren't just mud! There were also stones, twigs, and even a few feathers tucked here and there.

Shelly usually didn't like to get too close to muddy things. She preferred to stay purr-fectly clean! So she had planned to just take a quick look and not touch anything. But then she saw something very fin-teresting. There was a small, round rock sitting on top of the mound. It didn't look like it was part of the nest. In fact, it looked like someone had just dropped it on top.

The rock wasn't very different from others that Shelly had seen in Kittentail Cove. *But this one is from Flamingo Island,* she thought. It would make a paw-some reminder of this trip!

"Mom?" Shelly shouted. She wanted to ask if it was fine to take the rock.

But Mom was too far away!

Shelly sighed. *I guess I can ask her later,* she thought. She started to dive into the water. But then she stopped. She reached a paw out and grabbed the rock. She tucked it in her pocket and swam back to her friends.

It couldn't hurt to take just one little rock, could it?

When Shelly returned to her friends, Angel asked, "What were you doing?"

"You'll see," Shelly answered.

"Well, wherever you went," Coral said, "you're back just in time."

"Why?" Shelly asked.

"Because the flamingos are dancing!" Angel replied. "Look!"

The pink birds were in the water near the beach. They were marching along, all together, for a while. Then they went their own ways. Some of the birds were stretching their necks out and moving their heads side to side. Some poked a wing one way and a leg in another way.

Some flamingos stood tall with their wings out to the sides. Others had bent over and stuck their tails in the air. They flapped their wings straight up to the sky.

"Flamingos are very good dancers!" Shelly exclaimed.

Angel nodded. Coral said, "My book said flamingos know one hundred thirty-six dance moves."

"That's almost as many as I know," Angel joked. Everyone giggled.

The girls watched the flamingos dance until the sun began to set. "We should probably get back to camp," Coral said. She dove off the rock. Angel followed her.

Shelly was the last one to leave. She didn't want to look away from the beautiful pink birds. She wanted to try to remember this fur-ever! But Coral was right. It would be hard to find the camp underwater if it got too dark.

Then Shelly remembered the surprise

waiting for Angel and Coral at the camp. She smiled and dove into the water, too. "Who wants to race back?" she called out.

"I do!" Angel yelled. She laughed and raced off.

Shelly floated next to Coral and giggled. "Do you think we should tell her that she's going the long way?"

Coral shook her head. "We can tell her when we are back at camp!"

8

Angel might have been in a bad mood after losing their race, but Shelly knew how to make her feel better. As soon as she got to camp, she asked Mom where the pillows were. "Here," Mom whispered.

Shelly floated over to Coral. She kept her paws and the pillows behind her back. When Angel swam up, scowling, Shelly yelled, "Surprise!"

"Sending me the long way was certainly

a surprise," Angel grumbled. But then she and Coral saw what Shelly was holding.

"Pillows!" Coral exclaimed. "I thought we forgot them."

"Mom and I collected flamingo feathers to fill the pillowcases," Shelly said. "I thought these would be good enough for tonight."

"It's so soft!" Angel purred, hugging her new pillow. "This one is good enough for every night!"

"Thank you, Shelly," Coral said. "You saved the day."

"Actually," Angel said, giggling, "you saved the night!"

Shelly smiled. "I couldn't let anything ruin our trip," she said.

"And now," Mom said, "I have a special treat for all of you. I took some shrimp from the traps. And I got branches from the shore. I thought we could swim to the surface and build a fire."

"So we can roast the shrimp over the fire?" Shelly asked.

"Just like the scallops we roasted at Camp Sandcrab?" Angel added.

"Exactly!" Mom replied.

By the time the purrmaids were done eating, everyone was full, tired, and happy. The girls settled into their hammocks, snuggling their new flamingo-feather pillows. The full moon shone down through the mangrove roots and made the water glow.

"This has been a purr-fectly paw-some day," Coral said sleepily.

"I'm never going to fur-get it!" Angel added.

That's when Shelly remembered something. "I have to show you guys what I found today," she whispered. She took out the rock from the flamingo nests. "Look at this!"

"What is it?" Angel asked.

Shelly shrugged. "It's just a rock. But I thought I could decorate it at home. Then it would always be a reminder of this trip."

Coral looked carefully at the rock. "Are you sure you were allowed to take this?" she asked.

Shelly shrugged. "It's just a rock,"

she said. "I didn't think it would be a purr-oblem."

Coral took her book out of her bag. She flipped through the pages. Then she turned the book to show the others. "Doesn't that rock look like a flamingo egg?"

"We saw cracked eggshells near the flamingo nests," Shelly said. "All the eggs have hatched. This is just a rock."

"Shelly is probably right," Angel said.

Coral shrugged. "I guess so. I just got worried for a second."

"I think we've all had a long day," Shelly said. She put the rock under her pillow. "Let's get some sleep. There's still a lot to do tomorrow."

The girls said good night again. As Shelly closed her eyes, she thought, *It's definitely just a rock. Isn't it?*

When Shelly opened her eyes, it didn't look like morning. Everything around her was still dark. But something had clearly woken her up. She sat up in her hammock. She heard the sound again.

It must have woken Mom, too. "Did you hear that?" she asked, frowning. "It sounded like a flamingo chick to me."

Shelly lifted the corner of her pillow. Were the noises coming from the rock?

The purrmaids waited, but there were no other sounds. Mom shrugged. "Maybe I imagined it," she said, yawning. "I must have been dreaming about flamingos!"

Shelly didn't say anything.

"I'm awake," Mom continued, "so I'll bring the shrimp traps back. Get a little more rest, Shelly. You girls don't need to be up quite yet."

Mom swam away. Shelly lay back on her pillow. And then she heard it again! This time, she was sure the noise was coming from the rock! *Could this actually be an egg instead of a rock?*

"Coral! Angel!" Shelly shouted. "Wake up!"

"It can't be morning, can it? Already?" Coral mumbled.

"It's still dark!" Angel grumbled.

"You have to wake up," Shelly said. "There's a purr-oblem!"

Right away, Angel and Coral leapt out of their hammocks. "What is it?" Angel asked.

Shelly held out the egg-rock. Something inside made a chirping noise. "I think Coral was right," she said. "This isn't a rock!"

Angel's mouth dropped open. She didn't know what to say. Coral quickly grabbed her book again. She read for a minute. Then she said, "It says here that flamingo chicks start calling out to their parents for two or three days before they hatch."

Shelly gulped. *What have I done?*

9

It felt like it took Mom fur-ever to get back with the shrimp traps. When she finally arrived, Coral and Angel took the traps from her right away.

"Thank you, girls," Mom said. "You're being so helpful this morning!"

"Mom," Shelly said quietly, "there's something I have to tell you."

Mom's smile disappeared. "What is it, dear?" she asked.

"I know we weren't supposed to touch anything from Flamingo Island without asking," Shelly began. "But I didn't listen. I'm sorry, Mom."

Mom let out a deep breath. Then she smiled again. "I'm not happy that you didn't listen," she said, "but I am proud of you for being honest now. I know it isn't easy to be honest when you're worried about getting in trouble."

"Is she in trouble, Mrs. Lake?" Coral asked.

Mom shook her head. "No, she's not." She patted Shelly's shoulder. "It's really important that we try not to disturb wild animals and wild places. That's why it's a good rule to avoid taking anything. But the island won't be ruined if you grabbed one little leaf or seashell. So don't worry."

Shelly took a deep breath. "I didn't take a leaf. Or a seashell."

"What did you take?" Mom asked.

Shelly held out the flamingo egg. "I thought it was a rock," she said. "But there are noises coming from inside. I think this is a flamingo egg. And I think it's going to hatch soon!"

Mom's mouth dropped open. At first, she didn't say anything. Shelly felt tears welling in her eyes.

Angel floated closer to Shelly. She put a paw around Shelly's waist. "Shelly didn't mean to take an egg, Mrs. Lake," she purred. "It was an accident."

"I know it was," Mom said quietly. "But now we have to figure out what to do."

Shelly couldn't take it any longer. She began to cry. "I don't understand," she wailed. "You told me that I didn't need to ask permission all the time. That I'm old enough to think about things and figure out what to do by myself. But when I made a decision, it was the wrong one! I shouldn't have taken this without asking first!"

Mom sighed. "This is a tough one," she said. "You *are* supposed to be thinking through your actions. You *are* old enough to make decisions by yourself. That's just part of growing up." She touched Shelly's face with her paw. "But the thing is, even grown-ups make bad decisions sometimes. We make mistakes, too."

Shelly sniffed. "So what do I do now that I've made this mistake?" She looked down at the egg. "What do I do about this?"

"I don't know," Mom answered. When Shelly frowned harder, she held up a paw. "But we have some time. The baby flamingo is safe inside the egg."

"Even underwater?" Coral asked.

Mom nodded. "The baby chick will need air. But flamingo eggs are all right underwater."

"Don't worry, Shelly," Angel said. "I bet Mr. Nemo will know what to do."

"Do we have to tell him?" Shelly asked quietly. "He's going to think I'm really irresponsible."

"I don't think that's true," Mom said. "But we don't have to tell him that you're the one who took the egg. Not if you don't want to. We just need to ask him what to do now."

"Can't we just sneak up to the nest and put the egg back?" Shelly asked.

Mom shook her head. "We can't do anything that might scare the flock. And I don't know if the parents would be confused if they see us with the egg." She checked her watch. "The Trident will be here soon. I'm sure Mr. Nemo will have the answer."

"Let's get everything packed up," Coral suggested. "That way we'll be ready when Mr. Nemo gets here."

Angel used her pillow to make a little nest for the egg on the ocean floor. "Put it here while we pack up," she said.

Shelly placed the egg gently on the pillow. The chick inside the egg made another peep. "It's going to be all right, little one," she whispered. "I purr-omise we'll figure out how to get you back home."

The purrmaids quickly packed up the camp. "I think we got everything," Coral said. "Should we go wait for the Trident?"

Everyone nodded—except Shelly. She was staring at the egg. "Uh-oh!" she gasped. "Something is happening!"

"What?" Angel asked.

Shelly whispered, "We've got a new purr-oblem!" She lifted the egg in her paws. It shook for a moment. And then, a tiny crack appeared. "I don't think we can wait for Mr. Nemo! This chick could hatch any minute!"

10

The purrmaids left everything behind and raced toward the rocks. The area where the flamingos had been dancing yesterday was empty. The entire flock seemed to be gathered around the nests today.

The egg started to shake again. Shelly wanted to get to the nest quickly and put it back. *But if I do, the flamingos will see me! And then they might not believe this is their real baby!*

"We need a distraction!" Shelly exclaimed. "But what do we do?"

"Aren't they hungry?" Angel asked. "If they just went over to the shallows to eat, we could sneak this egg back."

Suddenly, Shelly had an idea. "Breakfast!" she exclaimed. "That's what we need."

"I think it's more important to get the egg home right now," Coral said.

"I don't mean breakfast for us," Shelly said. She turned to Mom. "The shrimp!" she cried. "We need a shrimp trap! Could you please go get one?"

Mom must have guessed Shelly's plan. In a flick of a tail, she dove toward the camp.

"What's the plan, Shelly?" Angel asked.

Shelly grinned. "We're serving those

flamingos the best breakfast they've ever had!"

"But I thought we weren't supposed to feed the flamingos," Coral said. "I thought we're supposed to leave them alone so they don't get confused about where to get food."

Shelly's smile fin-stantly disappeared. "I forgot that," she said quietly.

Mom had gotten back while Coral was asking her question. She was carrying a full shrimp trap. "I think we can make an exception just this once," she said.

Shelly's smile appeared again as Coral and Angel took the trap. "You two need to take the trap over there," she said. "Dump out all the shrimp into the shallows. Hopefully, the flamingos will smell them right away."

"And then they'll leave the nests to eat!" Angel said.

Shelly nodded. "While the birds are busy with breakfast, I'll get this little one home."

"You can count on us!" Coral said.

Each girl grabbed one side of the shrimp trap. They hurried to the golden beach. They dumped all the shrimp from the trap into the shallow water.

Shelly could smell the yummy shrimp already. But the flamingos didn't move!

Come on, Shelly thought. *Go get breakfast!*

Luckily, this time, Angel had a plan. She scooped up two pawfuls of shrimp. She swam underwater, toward the flamingos. She sprinkled the shrimp in the water along the way. When her paws were empty, she raced back to Shelly.

Coral copied what Angel did. By the time she was out of shrimp, the flamingos had noticed the swimming snacks. Coral even had to spin away to avoid a snapping beak!

"Nice moves, Coral!" Shelly exclaimed.

Coral grinned. "That was close!"

"Look!" Angel said, pointing. "It's working!"

One by one, the flamingos followed the line of shrimp, honking and flapping their wings. They circled the shrimp pile. In just a few minutes, the whole flock was happily chewing.

A soft noise came from the egg in Shelly's paws. "Now's your chance," Mom whispered.

Shelly took a deep breath. She glanced over to make sure the flamingos were still busy with their breakfast. Then she moved carefully toward the nest. "There you go, little one," she whispered. She placed the egg gently into the flamingo nest. "You're home again."

Suddenly, a crack appeared in the egg-shell. Shelly had to hurry! If the chick hatched and saw her before it saw its parents, it might think Shelly was its mother! She spun around and dove into the water as quickly as she could.

"Hurry, Shelly!" Angel whispered as Shelly swam back.

"The egg is about to hatch!" Coral added.

Shelly looked over at the nest. The egg was shaking again. Then a piece of egg-shell flew off the top. A little beak poked out. The chick began to chirp.

Most of the flamingo flock was still eating shrimp. But two of the flamingos had stopped. They raised their heads and looked at the egg. The chick peeped a few times. The two grown-ups pushed their way closer.

"Flamingo parents recognize their own chick's cries," Mom whispered. "I bet those are mom and dad!"

The flamingos reached the chick and honked happily. They flapped their wings and began to clean the chick's gray feathers.

"They're taking care of the baby!" Shelly purred. "We got the egg back in time!"

Shelly wanted to stay and watch the new chick for hours. But after a little while, Mom said, "It's time to go now. You know what Mr. Nemo said."

"The Trident leaves on time, no matter what," Shelly replied.

The purrmaids grabbed their bags and the rest of the shrimp traps from the camp. Soon, they were waiting at the Great Neptune Current.

Shelly said, "That was a real adventure! I just wish we found something to bring home."

"What are you talking about?" Angel said. "We have those paw-some pillows you made!"

Shelly scratched her head. "I forgot about those. I guess they're good reminders."

"Not just good," Coral said. "I'm going to put my pillow on my bed. I'll think of Flamingo Island every night before I fall asleep!"

"Me too!" Angel added.

Shelly reached down and felt her friendship bracelet with her other paw. "We didn't find a new charm, though."

"My pillow is almost as good as a charm," Angel said. She took her pillow out of her bag and gave it a squeeze. She squeezed out a few feathers by mistake!

"Be careful," Coral said. She scooped the feathers up. "Don't lose the stuffing."

"A few feathers don't make a difference," Angel said. "It's still snuggly."

Suddenly, Shelly had another idea. She took one of the feathers from Coral's paw. She held it against her bracelet. "Do you think we could use feathers as charms?"

"Brilliant!" Coral said. "They're the purr-fect reminder!"

"Shelly has saved the day again!" Angel exclaimed.

Shelly grinned. "I couldn't have done it without my best friends!"

The purrmaids have lots of friends around the ocean!

Read on for a sneak peek!

Early one morning in Seadragon Bay, a young mermicorn named Sirena could not sleep. She pushed the curtain on her window open. It was still dark outside! No one in the Cheval family would be awake yet.

Sirena fluffed her pillow. She pulled the blanket over her head. But she kept tossing and turning. *I'm too excited to sleep,* she thought. *What if today is the day?*

It was the first day of the season. For most mermicorns, that was just another day. But for all the colts and fillies in Seadragon Bay, it was special. That was when the Mermicorn Magic Academy invited new students to the school.

Magic was a part of mermicorn life. But like everything else, magic had to be learned. The best place for that was the Magic Academy. "I hope they pick me today!" Sirena whispered to herself. She finally gave up on sleeping. She floated out of bed and started to get dressed.

Sirena found her lucky blue top and put it on. She brushed out her long rainbow mane. She put on her favorite crystal earrings. Then she peeked out the window again. She could see some sunlight. *It's early,* she thought, *but maybe the mail is already here?*

Sirena swam toward the front door. She tried to be as quiet as a jellyfish. She didn't want to wake her family. But when she passed the kitchen, she saw that her parents were already up!

"Why are you awake?" Sirena asked.

Mom laughed. "Is that how you say good morning?"

Sirena sighed. "I'm sorry," she said. "I just wasn't expecting you. It's so early!" She swam to her parents and kissed their cheeks. "Good morning, Mom. Good morning, Dad."

"Good morning, Sirena," Dad neighed. "Are you hungry?"

Sirena nodded.

Dad started to put kelp pancakes on a plate. Mom floated over to Sirena. "So," Mom said, "today could be the day, right?"

Sirena nodded.

"That's why we're a

"The day a colt or f

join the Mermicorn M

big deal for parents," M

"I think a special day calls for a special breakfast," Dad said. His horn began to twinkle.